PORTRAITS
of LITTLE WOMEN

*A Gift
for Beth*

Don't miss any of the
Portraits of Little Women

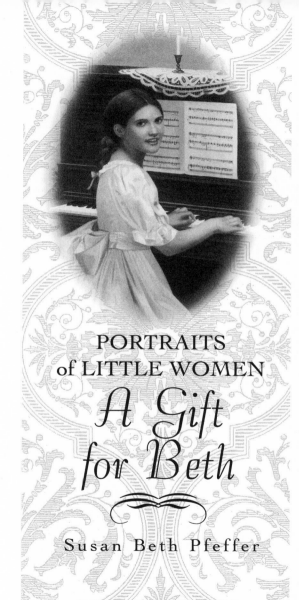

PORTRAITS
of LITTLE WOMEN

*A Gift
for Beth*

Susan Beth Pfeffer

DELACORTE PRESS

FOR AARON GOLDBLATT

Published by
Delacorte Press
a division of Random House, Inc.
1540 Broadway
New York, New York 10036

Copyright © 1999 by Susan Beth Pfeffer

Library of Congress Cataloging-in-Publication Data
Pfeffer, Susan Beth.
    Portraits of little women. A gift for Beth / Susan Beth Pfeffer.
      p.   cm.
    Based on characters found in Louisa May Alcott's Little women.
    Summary: Beth March receives a mysterious, but welcome, gift of new sheet music for the piano.
    ISBN 0-385-32667-X
    [1. Gifts—Fiction.   2. Piano music—Fiction.   3. Music—Fiction.]
I. Alcott, Louisa May, 1832–1888.   Little women.
II. Title.   III. Title: Gift for Beth.
PZ7.P44855Pjd   1999
[Fic]—dc21   98-45691
                                                CIP
                                                AC

The text of this book is set in 13-point Cochin.
Book design by Patrice Sheridan
Cover art © 1999 by Lori Earley
Text art © 1999 by Marcy Ramsey
Activities art © 1999 by Laura Maestro
Manufactured in the United States of America
May 1999
10 9 8 7 6 5 4 3 2 1
BVG

CONTENTS

PORTRAITS
of LITTLE WOMEN

A Gift
for Beth

CHAPTER 1

"You're doing better and better in school," Beth March said to her friend Sean O'Neill as they walked from school to the town of Concord one sunny May afternoon. "Soon you'll be the smartest boy in our class."

"I am already," said Sean, who was never shy about his accomplishments. "It's just the schooling I've been lacking. Not the brains, Miss Bethy."

Beth smiled. Sean had taken to calling her Miss Bethy when they'd first met and he'd been under the impression that she would expect him to show deference. But now they were friends — had been for months — and he called her that as a fond nickname.

"You should keep on with your schooling," Beth said. "You could become a lawyer or a doctor someday." She almost said "minister," which was what her father was. Her father was certainly the wisest man Beth knew. But Sean was a Roman Catholic, and Beth didn't think Catholics had ministers.

"My mam wants me to be a priest," Sean said. "She believes there's no higher calling."

"Then maybe that's what you should be," Beth replied.

Sean shook his head. "That's not the life for me," he declared. "I'm not one to give up the pretty lasses. No, I'm going to learn all I can, and then I'll go back to Ireland and help throw the Brits out of my homeland."

"We didn't like having them here, either," Beth said. "Maybe someday I could help you with your fight."

"You help me every single day," Sean said. "Finding work for my mam and me. Seeing to it my sisters have a roof over their heads and food in their bellies."

"Aunt March did all that," Beth said. "She's the one who hired your mother and gave you the job of helping her gardener. She's the one whose cottage your family is living in. I didn't do anything."

"That's not the way my mam tells it," Sean replied. "In her eyes, you're a little saint, Miss Bethy. Not a day goes by she doesn't tell Kathleen and Maggie that they should try to be as good as you, even if you are a godless heathen Protestant."

"Oh, dear," said Beth. "I'm really not that good. And I'm certainly not a godless heathen."

Sean laughed. "In me mam's eyes all the fine citizens of Concord are godless heathens," he said. "But you, at least, are a saint."

Beth laughed along with him. She couldn't help picturing Aunt March's reaction to being called a godless heathen. Not that she'd want to be anywhere near Aunt March should that ever happen.

"Do you have many errands to run in town?" Beth asked. She knew Sean had been told to pick up some things for Aunt March on his way home from school.

"Just a few items," he said. "Flour, soap, and a book your aunt requested from that Mr. Marshall."

"Let's start with him, then," said Beth. "His store is just a few doors down."

Beth loved going to Mr. Marshall's. He owned a handsome bookstore, and had a rule that a customer had to be at least ten years old before he'd let her in. Beth had turned ten recently, and ever since then, she'd taken every opportunity to go into the store. She never bought anything, though. Mr. Marshall's books were expensive, and what little money Beth had, she always seemed to need for other things. But just to be in the store, to breathe in the scent of the fine books, was enough for her. And as long as she kept quiet, Mr. Marshall didn't seem to mind. He was her father's friend and a particular friend of her older sister Jo, but Mr. Marshall had a temper, and on occasion he frightened Beth.

Today Beth was pleased to have an excuse to be in the bookstore, and she was glad Mr. Marshall liked Aunt March, who was one of his best customers. She was sure Mr. Marshall would be in a good mood.

"Oh, look," Beth said as they approached the store. "Mr. Marshall is selling sheet music now."

Mr. Marshall had put a large sign in his window. SHEET MUSIC, it read, and under the sign was the largest display of sheet music Beth had ever seen.

"How wonderful," she said. Just to see all those pieces of music made her happy. She loved playing the piano at home, and every evening, after supper, her parents and her sisters gathered around while she played their favorite hymns and songs. Everyone always sang along.

Having played the songs over and over, Beth knew all of them by heart. So it was a special treat to see dozens of new songs in Mr. Marshall's store.

"Aren't they beautiful?" Beth said as she stared wistfully at the window display. "I so wish I could learn one or two."

"What are they?" asked Sean. "Some kind of magazine?"

"No, they're the music to songs," Beth said. "With the lyrics as well. If I had one, I could play it on my piano, and Father, Marmee, and Meg, Jo, and Amy could all learn the words and sing along. It's a wonderful way to spend an evening or even a rainy day."

"I wouldn't know," said Sean. "The only piano I've ever seen has been at your house, Miss Bethy. Mrs. March doesn't care for music, and there's none in her parlor. Not that I'm spending a lot of time in the grand house."

"But you know songs," Beth said. "I've heard you whistle a few tunes, and even sing on occasion."

"Sure, and music is a part of every Irishman's life," said Sean. "But piano music is not.

When you're starving for a morsel of food, it's not piano music you're thinking of."

"But now you're not starving," Beth said. "I know you work hard for your food, but Aunt March feeds you well. Perhaps someday you could own a piano, a better one even than mine." She knew hers wasn't very good, but it didn't matter. The sound of her family singing was beautiful enough to her ears. "If you work hard, Sean," she added, "and stay in America, and don't go back to Ireland to throw the Brits out, you could be a rich man someday. If that's what you want."

"Is that what you think I should want?" asked Sean. "To give up all my dreams for the sake of a piano?"

"No, of course not. I just meant . . ." But Beth wasn't sure what she meant. "Never mind," she said instead. "I'm going to go into the store with you and see how much the sheet music costs."

"And have you the money for such fine things?" Sean asked.

Beth shook her head. "I haven't any money

at all," she admitted. "I spent my last few pennies on Monday, on sweets. But still, if I find out how much the music is, perhaps someday I'll be able to afford it."

"Or maybe Mr. Marshall will be making a gift of it to you," said Sean. If he'd been angry at Beth, his mood had passed. Sean was like Jo March that way, quick to anger. But unlike Jo's, his anger disappeared almost immediately.

The bell rang merrily as Beth and Sean entered the store. "Hello, Beth," Mr. Marshall said when he saw who his customers were. "I don't believe I know your friend."

"This is Sean O'Neill," Beth said. "He's the smartest boy in my class."

"Are you, now?" said Mr. Marshall. He looked Sean up and down.

"I am," said Sean, and Beth could see he was trying to decide whether Mr. Marshall was friend or foe.

"Sean works for Aunt March," Beth said. "And he's here to pick up a book for her."

"Certainly," Mr. Marshall said, and he

smiled at them. "The book is right here, waiting for someone to take it to Mrs. March. I trust she's all right."

"That she is," Sean said. "She just asked me to run some errands for her, and this is one."

"I'm always pleased to be an errand," said Mr. Marshall. He handed the book to Sean. "Is there anything else I can do for you?"

"Yes," Beth said. "The sheet music in your window. Is it terribly expensive?"

"I don't think so," Mr. Marshall replied. "A quarter each. Five for a dollar."

"Oh, dear," said Beth. Mr. Marshall might as well have said each piece was five dollars. Beth hadn't had a quarter of her own since Christmas. "I don't suppose . . ."

"Suppose what?" asked Mr. Marshall.

"What Miss Bethy is trying to say is, she don't suppose you might be offering her a piece of that fine sheet music as a gift," said Sean. "A token of friendship for such a sweet lass."

Mr. Marshall looked sadly at Beth. "*Et tu, Bethy?*" he said.

Had Mr. Marshall sneezed? "God bless you," Beth replied, just to be on the safe side.

"No, no," Mr. Marshall said. "Not *achoo*. *Et tu*. It's what Julius Caesar said to Brutus. *Et tu, Brute?* It means 'You too?' As in, even you, Beth, even you are trying to get something for free from me."

Sean stepped forward. "That's no way to be talking to Miss Bethy," he said. "She asked nothing of you and your thievin' bookshop."

"What did you just say?" said Mr. Marshall. "I think you'd best take the book and leave my store. I'm tired of all you children coming in and looking around, with no money to spend, and when you do have it, you spend it on candies and games anyway. From now on I'll have no children in this store, ever!"

"I'm sorry," Beth whispered.

"I'm not," said Sean, looking directly at Mr. Marshall. Before he could say more, Beth pulled him out of the store.

"He's a Brit, I can tell," Sean proclaimed loudly as he and Beth continued on their errands. "A stinking landlord, too, I'll be wagering."

"No, he isn't," Beth said. "He's just trying to earn a living. But he does scare me so."

"Then that's bad enough," said Sean. "For any godless heathen who scares Miss Bethy deserves an eternity in hell."

Beth shook her head sadly. If all the godless heathens who scared her spent eternity in hell, hell would be an overcrowded place indeed.

CHAPTER 2

"*I* know Sean is a friend of yours," Jo said that evening as the girls gathered in Meg and Jo's bedroom before going to bed. "But he does have a terrible temper."

Beth joined her sisters in laughter.

"What?" Jo asked. "What's the joke?"

"Merely that you have a temper of your own," said Meg. "You're no one to sound so self-righteous."

"You sounded like Aunt March," said Amy.

"Oh, that is cruel," said Jo, but she laughed as well. "I suppose it takes one to know one. And Mr. Marshall's temper is as fierce as mine or Sean's."

13

"Mr. Marshall really didn't get all that angry," said Beth. "Neither of them did. But he said something funny about Julius Caesar. '*Et tu,* Bethy?' "

"Oh, he didn't," Meg said, and then she laughed even more. "That was wicked of him."

"I don't understand," Amy said. "What does it mean?"

"Julius Caesar was assassinated by a group of Romans," Meg explained. "As he was being stabbed to death, Caesar recognized one of his assassins. It was his friend Brutus. When Caesar saw that he'd been betrayed, he said, '*Et tu, Brute?*' It means, 'You too, Brutus?' I suppose Mr. Marshall thinks we Marches are always after him for free books."

"We are," said Jo. "But he never gives us any. Still, I suppose he felt Beth was too sweet to ever ask him for anything. And it's true, Beth, you never do ask anything of anybody, and yet you're the one Mr. Marshall insults. It truly is unfair."

"I'm not sure how sweet I am," said Beth. "I would have asked Mr. Marshall if I'd had the courage. I very much wanted that sheet music. But I don't have a quarter to buy even one piece with."

"Don't look at me," said Amy. "I've three pennies to my name, and I'm saving them for new hair ribbons. It's terribly unfair how poor we are, when other girls have all the hair ribbons they could ever want and more."

"We're more than rich enough," said Beth. "Compared to the O'Neills, we're richer than Croesus. Now that it's planting season, Sean works every afternoon in the garden, and his mother scrubs and polishes for Aunt March six days a week, just so he and his sisters have enough to eat and clothes to wear. And that's a thousand times better than the way they were living when I first met them. Remember, Amy? They were half starved, and the shanty they lived in was drenched every time it rained. They wore rags and didn't have shoes. Don't ever say we're poor just because you don't have as many new hair ribbons as you'd like."

Amy sighed. "All right. I know there are

people worse off than we are. But that doesn't stop me from wanting more than I have."

"We always want more than we have," said Meg. "Everyone does. Even you, Beth. You'd like new sheet music."

"And I don't blame you," said Jo. "It must be tiresome for you, Bethy, playing the same songs night after night."

"It's certainly tiresome for me," said Amy.

Her sisters stared at her.

"All I meant was, I'd like to learn some of the newer, more fashionable songs," Amy declared. "I don't think there's been a new piece of music in this house since I was born."

"It would be nice to learn some of the newer songs," Meg admitted. "My friends all seem to know them, and I have to pretend to sing along. And I do love singing."

"Then we're agreed," said Jo. "Beth should · have some new music."

"Fashionable songs?" asked Amy.

"And why not?" said Jo. "My plays could stand a bit of new music themselves. Surely we have twenty-five cents amongst us."

"Three cents," Amy said. "And I really do need new hair ribbons."

Meg opened her purse. "Seven cents," she said. "I'd hate to give it all up, even for a fashionable new song, though."

"I spent my last penny on writing paper," Jo said. "I've nothing to offer except my bright ideas."

"I don't have any money either," said Beth. "So all we have is ten cents, and that would mean Amy and Meg would have to give up all their money, which neither one of them wants to do."

"Bother," said Jo. "I hate to admit it, but sometimes I feel just the way Amy does. I know we have more than enough, but it would be nice to have a few extra pennies to call our own."

"Do you think we could ask Marmee for the money?" said Amy. "I'm sure she and Father would enjoy it if Beth had new music to play."

"Of course we could ask them," said Meg. "But I know for a fact Marmee has two bolts of cloth on order to make summer dresses for you and Beth. And Father's trips to Boston are expensive. He's so very careful not to spend a penny more than he has to when he's there."

Jo nodded. "He never eats lunch when he's in Boston," she said. "I heard him discussing that once with Marmee. He eats only breakfast and trusts that someone will feed him supper. Do you think we should ask him for twenty-five cents for sheet music?"

"No," said Amy with a sigh. "Nor Marmee, either, since I desperately need a new dress. Your clothes are always in tatters by the time they come to me. It's very hard being the youngest."

"It's not easy being the oldest, either," said Meg. "I know I should be grateful for everything I have, but I look at my friends, and their lives seem so easy. They never want for anything. Twenty-five cents for a piece of sheet music would mean nothing to them, and to us, it's an insurmountable obstacle."

"Aunt March has plenty of money," said

Amy, "and sometimes she's generous and gives us a little."

"And most times she doesn't," Jo said.

Amy frowned. "It was just a thought."

"If Aunt March liked music, it might have worked," said Meg. "But she doesn't, and I can't picture her handing over twenty-five cents to Beth out of the goodness of her heart."

Beth was just as glad. She couldn't imagine herself asking Aunt March for the money. It was hard enough talking to Aunt March when she had to, without making a special trip to Aunt March's house just to beg.

"We all like the songs I know," she said, trying to brighten her sisters' spirits. "They're lovely songs, really. And maybe someday I'll learn some new ones, some fashionable ones."

"What's fashion to the Marches!" cried Jo. "We have no need of fashion."

"Speak for yourself," Amy muttered.

"I am," Jo admitted, and the four sisters burst into laughter once again.

CHAPTER 3

Beth lingered in front of Mr. Marshall's store window that Monday. All weekend long, she'd thought about the music she would never learn. Seeing it in the window made her feel both happy and sad. Happy to know the music existed, sad to know she'd never be able to afford it.

"Beth! Beth March!"

Beth looked up and saw Mr. Marshall standing at the door.

"Come in, Beth," he said. "I need to talk to you."

Beth was reasonably sure she'd done nothing wrong. She might not be allowed in the store anymore, but she couldn't remember Mr. Marshall forbidding her to look at his window.

"Thank you," said Mr. Marshall as Beth followed him inside. "I was hoping I'd see you today."

"Why?" Beth asked. Mr. Marshall had never wanted to see her before.

"There's been a terrible misunderstanding," said Mr. Marshall, "between Mrs. March and myself."

"Marmee?" Beth asked. She couldn't imagine her mother misunderstanding anything. Marmee always understood just what each of her daughters was feeling.

"Not that Mrs. March," Mr. Marshall said. "Your aunt, Mrs. March."

"Oh, Aunt March," Beth said. Aunt March certainly was capable of misunderstanding many things.

"I got this note from her today," Mr. Marshall explained. "It seems that servant boy you were with the other day has filled her ears with lies about me."

"Sean?" asked Beth. "Sean wouldn't lie."

"There are lies and there are lies," said Mr. Marshall. "I'm not suggesting he told Mrs. March I was a murderer. Just that I was rude to you. Which I don't believe I was. And that I was insulting to him as well. Which I don't remember being either."

"Sean takes offense easily," Beth said. "Because of the Brits who've taken over his homeland. Sean's from Ireland, you know."

"I guessed as much," said Mr. Marshall. "And the Irish have a great way with storytelling. He must have told Mrs. March that I was the devil incarnate, for in her note she says she regrets that she'll never do business with me again because of how I treated you and this Sean. I must admit I'm surprised Mrs. March cares that much about one of her servants."

"Sean's more than just a servant to Aunt March," Beth said. "His mother works for Aunt March as well, and Aunt March has given clothes to the O'Neills and seen to it that the children all go to school. That includes

Sean, even though he's apprenticed to her gardener and old enough to work full-time."

"That's all very interesting," Mr. Marshall said. Beth knew that meant he didn't find it interesting at all. "But where does that leave me? Mrs. March believes the boy's lies and threatens never to do business with me again. She's one of my best customers. Beth, you were here when the boy picked up the book for Mrs. March. You have to visit her and tell her exactly what happened."

"But what did happen?" Beth asked. "If I remember correctly, I came into the store and asked how much the sheet music was, and then you chased Sean and me away and told us never to come into your store again."

"I grant you, it might have seemed like that," Mr. Marshall said. "I'd had a very difficult day here, Beth. One of my customers had tried to return a book, claiming it was tea-stained when she'd bought it, and of course she was the one who'd spilled the tea all over it. She must have been responsible, since the

23

book was brand new. Then a delivery came without three books I'd requested and with two I hadn't asked for. And during the course of the day, five different people came into the store, spent hours staring at all the titles, and then left without making a single purchase. One of them even had the nerve to complain about the books I carried. Not enough romances. Too many serious texts. It's a hard life being a bookseller, Beth. I should have taken my mother's advice and sold groceries instead. People always need flour and sugar and spices. They don't just read the labels and walk away empty-handed."

"Then why don't you sell groceries," Beth asked, "if you'd be happier doing it?"

"Because I love books," Mr. Marshall said with a sigh. "It's my customers I don't always love. My ideal customer would be a man like your father, Beth, only with money. Still, I'm fortunate to have his friendship, and that of your neighbor, Mr. Emerson, as well. My concern is that Mrs. March will fill their ears with outrageous stories of my misconduct and they'll also cease doing business with me."

"That would be terrible," Beth agreed.

"And that's why you must talk to your aunt," Mr. Marshall said. "Tell her the truth. Tell her I was a bit short-tempered with you and the servant boy."

"His name is Sean," Beth said. "Sean O'Neill. It's a fine Irish name."

"Sean, then," Mr. Marshall said. "The smartest boy in your class. See, Beth, I listen to what you say. Tell Mrs. March that it was a natural misunderstanding and I meant no disrespect to you or to Sean. You will do that for me, won't you? You could pay her a visit this very afternoon and then come back here and reassure me that Mrs. March understands what happened. She must forgive me. And, of course, I hope she'll keep on doing business with me. Please, Beth. I know it's a great deal to ask of you, but my very livelihood depends upon it."

Beth looked at Mr. Marshall. She was unaccustomed to having adults make such serious demands of her. Mostly they didn't seem to notice she existed, which was just the way she liked it.

"Aunt March frightens me," she murmured.

"She's a powerful woman," Mr. Marshall said. "But I'm sure she loves you dearly, Beth. You are her great-niece, after all, and family counts to a woman like that."

Beth knew that was true. Her aunt was always bemoaning the behavior of Father and Marmee and Beth and her sisters for not living up to the great March name.

"It means that much to you?" she asked.

"It does," Mr. Marshall said. "I'd go with you myself, Beth, but I can't afford to leave the store. Someone might actually come in and buy a book for a change. Beth, do this for me and I'll be eternally in your debt."

Mr. Marshall looked so desperate that Beth knew she would have to agree. "Very well," she said. "But I won't say Sean lied. I'm sure he didn't."

"Then he must not have," said Mr. Marshall. "That's what a misunderstanding is, after all. Something not properly understood. Thank you, Beth. And don't forget to come back here once you've paid your call and tell me all is forgiven. I won't be able to sleep tonight until I hear from you that all is well again."

"I promise I'll come back," Beth said. She left the store and began the long walk to Aunt March's. She dreaded the idea of calling on her aunt. And to visit her for the sole purpose of making peace between Aunt March and Mr. Marshall because of something Sean had said truly made Beth nervous.

Why couldn't Beth have been in the store with Amy instead of with Sean? Amy had a way of charming all who knew her and getting just what she wanted. Or Meg. If Beth had gone to the store with Meg, Mr. Marshall would have been far friendlier. Meg was a young lady already, and people treated her that way. And Jo and Mr. Marshall swapped stories about their tempers and the trouble they got them into. If Beth had gone to the store with Jo, Mr. Marshall never would have gotten angry and accused Beth of attempting to assassinate him.

But it had to be Sean, Beth thought. Sean, who saw everybody as the enemy until they proved themselves otherwise.

But Beth knew it was unfair to blame her predicament on Sean. It was her own fault for wanting what she couldn't have. Sean only wanted what he could see Beth yearned for. It was Beth's greed, and hers alone, that was forcing her to pay an unexpected call on Aunt March.

"I'll never want what I can't have again," Beth vowed, but she knew that vow would be close to impossible to keep. "I'll never let anyone know what I want if I can't have it," she whispered, but then she thought of a lifetime of secrets kept from Jo and Meg and Amy and Father and Marmee and knew that was impossible as well.

"I'll only let my family know what I dream of," she said, and that was a promise she knew she had a fighting chance of keeping.

Of course, Aunt March was family. And for Beth to clear up any misunderstanding, Aunt March would have to be told of Beth's greedy desire for the sheet music. And even if Beth could clear things up between Aunt March and Mr. Marshall, she knew Aunt March would never approve of a family that couldn't afford twenty-five cents for a trifle, or of a girl who wanted twenty-five cents for a new song to learn.

Beth sighed. None of this was Aunt March's fault, or Mr. Marshall's, or Sean's. It was her fault and hers alone. But that didn't make the idea of talking to Aunt March any more appealing.

CHAPTER 4

"Why, Miss Beth," Mrs. O'Neill said, opening Aunt March's door. "Do come in. Is your aunt expecting you?"

"No, she isn't," Beth said. "Where's Williams?" Williams was Aunt March's butler, and he usually opened the door to guests.

"Ah, the poor man," said Mrs. O'Neill. "A terrible stomach pain he's suffering. Mrs. March told him to stay in bed until he's better. She's a fine woman, Miss Beth. She works you hard, but she works you fair."

"I'm glad this job has turned out so well,"

Beth said. "Sean's doing better and better at school. And Kathleen and Maggie seem so happy when I see them."

"And why shouldn't they be happy?" their mother asked. "With food in their bellies and decent clothes on their backs? Maggie says she doesn't much care for school, and Mrs. March has already offered to take her on here. Maybe one day she'll be a fine lady's maid."

"I'm so pleased," Beth said. "Is my aunt busy? I really do have to see her."

"Then see her you will, although there's a gentleman with her now," said Mrs. O'Neill. "Stay where you are, Miss Beth, and I'll be making the announcement."

"Not if she has company," Beth said, but there was no stopping Mrs. O'Neill. Beth sighed. Aunt March would certainly be in no mood to see her if she already had a caller.

"You're to go right in," said Mrs. O'Neill, bustling out of the front parlor. "And be sure to come to the kitchen when your visit is over, Miss Beth. There's some lovely little cakes just waiting for you to take home."

"Thank you," Beth said. She entered the front parlor and found Aunt March and a distinguished-looking gentleman sharing a pot of tea.

The gentleman rose as Beth walked in. Beth blushed. She knew gentlemen were expected to rise when a lady entered, but no one had ever treated her like a lady before.

"Beth," said Aunt March. "Mr. Laurence, this is my great-niece, Beth March. Beth, Mr. Laurence. He has recently moved to Concord. In fact, he's a neighbor of yours. He and I have known each other for many years."

"It's a pleasure to meet you, Miss March," Mr. Laurence said.

"Thank you," Beth mumbled. New people terrified her, but she suspected that even if she'd known Mr. Laurence for many years, he'd have the same effect on her. He was a large man with gray hair and piercing blue eyes.

"Speak up," Aunt March said. "I'm sure Mr. Laurence and I are both interested in your reason for calling."

"Take a seat, Beth," Mr. Laurence said, sitting down.

"Yes, do sit down." Aunt March pointed to a chair. "We can ring for another cup if you'd like some tea."

"No, thank you," Beth said. "I really can't stay very long."

"Then speak your piece," Aunt March said. "If you're here to tell me how badly Mr. Marshall treated you, I already know. Sean O'Neill told me all about it when he brought me the book. I sent Mr. Marshall a letter informing him of my intention to sever our business relationship. I will not have my family spoken to rudely, nor my servants."

"I'm here because of Mr. Marshall," Beth said, "but not to tell you how badly he behaved."

"Why, then?" Aunt March asked. "Explain yourself."

"Mr. Marshall didn't really behave badly," Beth said.

"Are you accusing Sean of lying?" Aunt March asked.

"No, of course not," Beth said. "It was all just a misunderstanding, Aunt March. Mr. Marshall said something about Brutus, and we didn't know what he meant, and Sean just naturally assumed it was an insult. Sean's very protective of me, you know."

"And rightly so," Aunt March declared. "He's a smart lad, and I doubt he'll be satisfied to work as a gardener's apprentice much longer. Perhaps someday he'll go out west. In the territories, a man's past is never held against him. Sean could do well for himself in a place like that."

"I must admit I'm confused," Mr. Laurence said. "What does Brutus have to do with anything?"

"He assassinated Julius Caesar," Beth said. "Have you heard of him?"

Mr. Laurence smiled. "Yes, I believe I have."

"Well, Mr. Marshall compared me to him," Beth said. "Brutus, that is. Because I wanted some sheet music."

"Ah, yes," Mr. Laurence said. "Brutus was well known for his fondness for music."

"Was he?" Beth asked. "I'm afraid I never heard of him before Mr. Marshall mentioned him."

"Mr. Laurence is joking," Aunt March said. "He is simply puzzled as to why Mr. Marshall would compare you to Brutus."

"Because I wanted the sheet music," Beth said. "He had it in his shop window, and it made me realize how much I'd love to learn some new pieces. I play the piano, Mr. Laurence, but I haven't had too many chances to learn new songs. When I saw the sheet music and went into the store with Sean, Mr. Marshall got the idea that I'd like him to give me the sheet music. It was twenty-five cents for a single piece, and I don't have twenty-five cents."

"Beth March," Aunt March said. "Did you beg Mr. Marshall for that music?"

"No, Aunt March," Beth said. "It was all a misunderstanding. But it wasn't Mr. Marshall's fault any more than it was Sean's. So please forgive Mr. Marshall, since he didn't do anything wrong. He sent me here to explain just what happened because I was there, and, truly, my feelings weren't hurt."

"Well, well," Aunt March said. "Mr. Laurence, what do you think I should do?"

"I think you should accept your niece's version of the events," he said. "For she was the injured party, and if she bears no grudge, I see no reason why you should."

"I agree," Aunt March said. "And I admit to some relief. Mr. Marshall's shop has been a great pleasure to me. He carries an excellent variety of books and a fine selection of papers and magazines."

"And sheet music, it would seem," said Mr. Laurence.

"That's of no interest to me," Aunt March said. "I have no ear for music. Do you care for it, Mr. Laurence?"

"Very much," he said, "although I have no gift for it."

"Beth is musical," Aunt March said. "Presumably from her mother's side of the family, since none of the Marches has ever been so inclined. Still, music is an asset for a young lady, and heaven knows my nieces can use all the advantages they can get."

"I'm sure they have many other advantages," Mr. Laurence said, "if this charming young lady is an example of the others."

Aunt March sniffed. "There are four of them, and each is different from the others," she said. "But there's hope for one or two of them, I suppose."

Mr. Laurence laughed. "How modest you are," he said. "Most women exaggerate the virtues of their family. I find your attitude quite refreshing."

"Very well," Aunt March said. "Beth, you may return to Mr. Marshall and tell him all is forgiven. Go to the kitchen and help yourself to some cakes. Mrs. O'Neill baked them last night, and I must say she has a real gift for baking."

"Thank you, Aunt March," Beth said. She was relieved to be excused and scurried happily away.

"Did you conclude your business with your aunt?" Mrs. O'Neill asked as Beth entered the kitchen.

"Yes, I did," Beth said. "Please tell Sean he shouldn't worry about Mr. Marshall and what he said. Mr. Marshall sometimes says things that he doesn't really mean."

"My Sean told me," Mrs. O'Neill said. "What a shame it was that man didn't give you a piece of that music you so wanted."

"He can't just give away his sheet music," Beth said. "He needs to sell it to make money and stay in business."

"You're a little saint, Beth March," Mrs. O'Neill said. "Seeing the best in everyone."

Beth shook her head sadly. "I wish I were," she said. "But I'm full of failings, Mrs. O'Neill."

"I'll hear none of that," said Mrs. O'Neill.

"Now take your cakes and give my regards to your kind mother and father. They're fine people, Miss Beth."

"I know," Beth said, taking the cake-laden basket. "Thank you, Mrs. O'Neill. And say hello to Sean and Kathleen and Maggie for me. Tell Sean I'll see him in school tomorrow."

"That I will, Miss Beth," Mrs. O'Neill said.

Beth smiled. As much as she'd dreaded her call on Aunt March, she had to admit things had gone quite well. And Mr. Marshall, she knew, would be happier still.

CHAPTER 5

"There's a package for you," Hannah said to Beth when Beth and her sisters arrived home from school the next day.

"A package?" Beth asked the March family housekeeper. She couldn't remember ever having received a package before.

"Well, where is it?" Amy asked.

"Yes, Hannah, don't hide it," Jo said. "Let's see what our Bethy got."

"This is so exciting," Meg said. "A surprise package. I wish someone would send me something special."

"Your day will come soon enough, I'm sure," Hannah said. "Here it is, Beth."

"Oh," Amy said. "It's just an envelope. I thought it would be big and thrilling."

"I like things that come in envelopes," Jo said. "Open it, Beth, and tell us what it is and who it's from."

Beth opened the envelope. "Oh, look," she said. "I can't believe it. It's sheet music."

"Indeed," Jo said. "A new song for you to learn, Beth."

Beth looked at her older sister. "Did you get it for me?" she asked.

"I wish I could say I did," Jo replied. "But you know I haven't a penny to my name."

"I can't claim credit either," Meg said.

"Don't look at me," Amy said. "I'm still saving for hair ribbons."

"Marmee," Jo said. "This is just the sort of surprise she'd think of. Although I don't know why she'd have it delivered and not carry it home. It isn't as though sheet music weighs anything."

"Where is Marmee?" Beth asked Hannah.

"In the garden," Hannah replied.

Beth ran outside to the garden, followed by her sisters. "Marmee, thank you," she said, waving the sheet music in the air. "This is such a wonderful surprise."

"Yes, I saw that you'd received a package," Marmee said, looking up from her planting. "What is it, Beth?"

"Sheet music," Beth said. "You mean you didn't buy it for me?"

"No, dearest, I didn't," Marmee replied. "I know nothing about it."

"Beth has a secret admirer," Amy said. "Some handsome young man who is wooing her through music."

"Amy, don't joke," Jo said. "Beth, have you any idea who sent you the music?"

Beth thought a moment. "I don't," she said. "If Marmee didn't give it to me, and none of you did either, I can't imagine who might have."

"Father, maybe?" Jo asked.

Marmee shook her head. "He's been in Boston for three days now," she said. "And I'm afraid his mind has been on abolition and not music."

"It certainly is a mystery," Jo said.

"No," Meg said. "It's no mystery at all."

Marmee and Meg's sisters all stared at her.

"It must have come from Aunt March," she said.

"Aunt March?" Jo asked.

"Aunt March," Meg repeated. "Beth, didn't you tell us Aunt March said music was an asset for a young lady?"

Beth nodded.

"I suppose Aunt March might have bought it," Jo said. "She certainly worries about our making good matches. Perhaps she thought twenty-five cents was a small amount to invest in Beth's marital future."

"What do you think, Marmee?" Beth asked.

"I don't know," Marmee replied. "But I suppose it's possible. Aunt March does get ideas in her head sometimes, and she might have thought a new piece of sheet music was a good idea for Beth."

"You'll have to go and thank her," Meg said.

"I know." Beth sighed. Two calls on Aunt March in two days. It was astounding how much trouble the sheet music was causing.

Beth's sisters offered to go with her, but Beth declined. If Aunt March was kind enough to give her such a thoughtful gift, Beth knew she shouldn't feel as though she needed protection.

She knocked on Aunt March's door and was pleased to see Williams open it. "Hello, Williams," she said. "I'm glad to see you're feeling better."

"Thank you, Miss Beth," Williams said. "Is your aunt expecting you?"

"I don't know," Beth said. "Is she in?"

"She is," Williams said. "I'll announce you."

Beth waited until Williams summoned her into the parlor.

"Two visits in two days," Aunt March said as Beth entered. "Of course, yesterday you were Mr. Marshall's emissary. To what do I owe today's visit, Beth?"

"I've come to thank you."

"You're welcome, of course," Aunt March said. "You enjoyed the cakes, then?"

"Oh, yes," Beth said. "Thank you for them as well."

"As well as what?" Aunt March asked.

"As well as the sheet music," Beth said, swallowing nervously.

"And what sheet music would that be?" Aunt March asked.

"I . . . I . . . that is to say," Beth began. "I mean, I thought you sent me some sheet music."

"And why should you think that?"

"The package came with no name on it," Beth said. "We naturally assumed you had sent it. Marmee didn't buy the sheet music, and Father's in Boston, and Meg and Jo and Amy couldn't possibly afford such a gift, so we were sure you must have."

"Because you ran out of other possibilities?"

inquired Aunt March. "There's no other reason, I gather."

"Should there be another reason?" Beth asked.

Aunt March gave Beth a look. "I have, over the years, been generous to your family," she said. "Although I gather you've never noticed."

"Of course I've noticed," Beth said. "And believe me, we've always appreciated all you've done for us. But I know you don't care for music, and that's why you weren't the first person I thought of."

"You're a smart girl, Beth," Aunt March said. "Quiet, but smart."

"Thank you." Beth couldn't remember Aunt March's ever praising her before.

"Don't be *too* smart," Aunt March said. "A little intelligence is an attribute in a young lady, but too much discourages men."

"I'll keep that in mind," Beth said. "Well, if it wasn't you who gave me the music, I'll still have to find out who did."

"Perhaps it was Mr. Laurence," Aunt March suggested. "He mentioned to me how much he enjoyed your company yesterday."

"Oh, dear," Beth said. "I suppose that means I have to pay him a call as well."

"It does indeed," Aunt March said. "Go, Beth. And take my advice."

"Yes, Aunt March?"

"Don't act as though he were the last person you thought of," Aunt March said. "Mr. Laurence is a fine man, but he's not as softhearted as I."

"I'll be careful," Beth said, but inwardly she shuddered. Paying a call on Mr. Laurence, even to thank him, was going to be even harder than calling on Aunt March.

CHAPTER 6

Beth went home first. She needed support before making another thank-you visit.

"It wasn't Aunt March," she said glumly to her sisters and Marmee as soon as she entered the parlor.

"It wasn't?" Meg asked. "I was so sure."

"It's still a mystery, then," said Jo. "I love a mystery."

"Aunt March thinks it must have been Mr. Laurence," Beth said.

"Mr. Laurence?" Marmee asked. "The gentleman who's moved in next to us?"

Beth nodded. "He was visiting Aunt March

when I told her about Mr. Marshall," she replied. "And he did appear to like music. Besides, who else could it be?"

"Then you'll have to visit Mr. Laurence to thank him," Marmee said. "Are you on your way over now?"

"I suppose so," Beth said. "Marmee, I don't want to go alone."

"I'll go with you," Amy offered. "I'd love to see the inside of his home."

"Don't be a goose," Jo said. "Beth doesn't need you snooping around while she says her thanks. I'll go instead."

"Would that be all right, Marmee?" Beth asked. "I would be so much happier if Jo came along."

"It's not the normal procedure, but I see no harm in it," Marmee said. "Don't overstay your welcome. I know Mr. Laurence slightly, and he is a very busy gentleman."

"Believe me, we'll be in and out," said Jo. "Come, Beth, let's get this call over with."

Beth gratefully followed her older sister out of the house. Jo was afraid of nothing and no one. Even Aunt March didn't scare her. As long as Jo was by her side, Beth knew she would be all right.

She felt that way until Mr. Laurence's butler opened the door. Williams no longer frightened her, because she was used to him, but this butler was far more imposing, and Beth felt far less secure.

"We're here to see Mr. Laurence," Jo said, while Beth remained silent. "Would you tell him that Miss Beth March and Miss Jo March are paying a call?"

"Is Mr. Laurence expecting you?" the butler asked.

Even Jo looked a little nervous. "No," she admitted. "But I'm sure he'll be pleased to see us. Beth in particular. He might even be expecting her."

The girls waited in the front hallway until the butler summoned them. The house was even grander than Aunt March's, and Beth became increasingly nervous.

"Please," she whispered to Jo. "You talk for me. I don't think I'll be able to say a word."

"If that's what you want," Jo whispered back. "But I'm sure there's nothing to be scared of. Mr. Laurence did you a good deed. He'll be delighted you've come to thank him."

But Beth had her doubts, and they only multiplied when the butler returned.

"Mr. Laurence has told me to say you may visit very briefly," the butler said. "He's involved in some work right now and cannot have a lengthy interruption."

"We won't be but a moment," Jo said, but she sounded considerably less confident than she had when alone with Beth.

The two girls followed the butler into the library.

"Christopher Columbus," Jo whispered. "There are more books here than Father and Mr. Emerson have combined."

Mr. Laurence was sitting at his desk, his back to the girls. When the butler announced them, he turned to face them. He looked far more imposing than he had in Aunt March's parlor.

"Yes?" he asked, but it sounded more like "no."

"We're here, that is, Beth's here, so to speak; well, we're both here, I suppose, to thank you," Jo stammered.

"Thank me?" Mr. Laurence asked. "For what, may I ask?"

Jo exchanged a panicked look with Beth. "The music," she said.

"Music?"

"The sheet music," Jo said. "You did send a piece of sheet music to Beth, didn't you?"

Mr. Laurence shook his head. "I know nothing about this. If that's all you came for, I suggest you go home."

"Yes, sir," Beth squeaked, turning to go.

But Jo stood still. "Are you sure you didn't send Beth the sheet music?" she asked.

"I believe I would know if I had," Mr. Laurence declared. "Now, if you'll excuse me, I have work to do."

"But if you didn't, who did?" Jo asked.

Beth knew Jo wasn't really expecting an answer from Mr. Laurence. In fact, she knew Jo wasn't really even asking him the question. She was simply thinking out loud. But Mr. Laurence was clearly getting more and more annoyed.

"Jo, we have to go," Beth whispered.

"I know," Jo said, but her eyes were on the books. She sighed. "I have never seen such a splendid library," she said.

"And you will never see it again if you don't leave immediately," Mr. Laurence barked. "I trust I've made myself clear."

"You have, sir," Beth said. "We're truly sorry. Really we are. Come, Jo." And she practically pulled Jo out of the library.

"I'm sorry," Jo said as they walked back to the March house. "I was simply transfixed by all those books. I was sure I could solve the mystery if I stayed in that room."

No one in the March household loved books the way Jo did. For all Beth knew, Mr. Laurence's library would have helped Jo figure out who'd sent the sheet music.

"Maybe some other time," Beth said.

Jo shook her head. "I'll never be allowed back in that house," she said. "I can be such a fool sometimes."

Beth stood absolutely still. "And so can I," she said.

"You?" Jo asked.

"Me," Beth said. "And you, and Marmee, and Meg, and Aunt March."

"Aunt March I can believe," said Jo. "But Marmee and the rest of us?"

"All of us," Beth said. "If I want to find out who sent me the sheet music, all I need to do is ask Mr. Marshall."

"Mr. Marshall." Jo nodded. "Of course. You don't even need to ask him. You can simply thank him."

"Oh, you don't think Mr. Marshall sent me the music, do you?" Beth asked. "He hates to give away things from his shop."

"But think of how much business you've saved him by convincing Aunt March that he did nothing wrong," Jo said. "The least he can do is give you a single piece of sheet music."

"But there was no note from him," Beth pointed out.

"He probably didn't see the need to include one," Jo reasoned. "Mr. Marshall wouldn't have known exactly what you told Aunt March. And he wouldn't have known Mr. Laurence was there. He simply assumed you would know the music came from him. Come, Beth. There's still time to go to his shop and give him your thanks."

"All right," Beth said. She only wished she were as sure as Jo that Mr. Marshall was her secret benefactor. But whether he was or not, he would certainly know who had been.

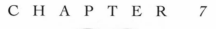

" *I*t's the March girls," Mr. Marshall said as Beth and Jo entered his shop. "Or two of them, at least. To what do I owe this honor?"

"At least he thinks it's an honor," Jo muttered. Beth surpressed a laugh.

"I've come to thank you," Beth said.

"You're welcome, I'm sure." Mr. Marshall smiled. "May I be so bold as to ask what for?"

"For the sheet music," Beth said. "You did have it sent to my house, didn't you?"

"That I did. I helped with the selection too."

"Helped?" Jo asked. "You didn't send the gift?"

"Why should I have done that?"

"Because Beth interceded for you with Aunt March," Jo said. "I was certain you were the one."

"If you didn't give me the sheet music, who did?" Beth asked.

"Didn't I include the note?" Mr. Marshall asked. He paused for a moment and looked at his counter. "You know, I didn't. The shop got busy for a while, and I forgot to attach the note with the music. Here, Beth. This should identify the giver."

"Who's it from?" Jo asked before Beth even had the note in her hand.

"Let me read it first," Beth said. She took the note from Mr. Marshall and read it eagerly.

Dear Miss Bethy,

My mother and Maggie and Kathleen and I all thought you would enjoy some new music to play.

Your respectful servant,

Sean O'Neill

"It was the O'Neills," Beth said.

"The O'Neills?" Jo asked.

"Is that their name?" Mr. Marshall asked. "The servant—I mean your friend Sean—and a woman he kept calling 'Mam' came in and asked for my help with the selection. I have to admit, I was surprised they had twenty-five cents between them, but they did. Mostly pennies, but it added up to twenty-five cents. They were uncertain which piece to purchase, but I was fairly sure I knew your taste, and I offered them several selections. Sean's mam, Mrs. O'Neill, as you say, didn't seem to be able to read, but Sean had no trouble, and between the two of them, they made their selection. Then Sean wrote the note, which I told him I'd include in the envelope, and which I didn't. And that's the complete story."

"Sean and his mother," Jo said. "I never would have guessed it was them."

"And Maggie and Kathleen," Beth said. "Oh, Jo. They must be so angry at me for not having thanked them already."

"Then we must run over to Aunt March's

and find them," Jo said. "Good day, Mr. Marshall."

"Good day to you, too, girls," he said. "And
please extend my apologies to the O'Neills for
forgetting to put in their note."

"I will," Beth said. She and Jo left the shop.
"Oh, Jo," she said. "I feel so terrible."

"They'll forgive you." Jo patted Beth's arm.
"Besides, it wasn't your fault. You've been
thanking people all over the place because of
Mr. Marshall's carelessness. There was no reason for you to assume the O'Neills would do
something so generous."

"But that's why I feel terrible," Beth said.
"The O'Neills have no money. I know Aunt
March pays them, but they work so hard and
they have so little. How can I possibly accept a
gift from them? I'll go home, return the sheet
music to Mr. Marshall, and ask him for the
twenty-five cents back to give to the O'Neills."

"You can't do that," Jo said. "You have to
accept their gift. It was important to them to
give you something they knew you would ap-
preciate."

"Then I'll have to give them something of equal value," Beth said. "But I have nothing."

"Oh, Bethy," Jo said. "Gifts aren't like that."

"Then what are they like?" Beth asked.

"What I mean is, you don't give a gift demanding anything in return," Jo said. "Well, Amy probably does, but that's simply her nature. The rest of the world isn't like that. Think of all you did for the O'Neills when you first met them. You gave them all your money and two of your dolls and your clothes and food. Did you expect them to give you anything in return?"

"Of course not," Beth said. "But even if I had, they had nothing to give."

"And now they do," said Jo. "Twenty-five cents is a lot to them. It's a lot to us, and we have so much more than they. But, Bethy, they wanted to show you how grateful they are and how much they care about you."

"Then you're saying I should simply thank them?" Beth frowned. "Still, there must be something I can do to show my appreciation for what they did."

"Marmee will know," Jo said. "Let's stop off at home first and get her opinion."

The girls walked home at a rapid pace. They found Marmee setting the table for supper.

"We found out who gave Beth the sheet music," Jo said, "and it wasn't Mr. Laurence."

"Then who was it?" Marmee asked, looking up from the table. Meg and Amy joined them in the dining room.

"It was the O'Neills," Beth said. "Sean wrote a note, but Mr. Marshall forgot to include it. Marmee, what should I do?"

"Thank them right away," Marmee said. "They must be wondering why you haven't already."

"But I want to do something more," Beth said. "Twenty-five cents is a fortune to them, Marmee. What can I possibly give them in return?"

"I've already told Beth she doesn't have to give them anything," Jo said. "But Beth is determined."

"Maybe she could give them one of her dolls," Meg suggested. "You have some nice ones, Beth, and I'm sure Maggie and Kathleen would enjoy getting another one from you."

"Sean wouldn't care for a doll," Amy said. "Beth, don't you have anything you could give them that they'd all like?"

"I haven't been able to think of a thing," Beth said. "Marmee, do you have any ideas?"

"Let me think for a moment," Marmee said. Her daughters fell silent as they watched their mother concentrate.

"I have it," Marmee said. "What did the O'Neills give you, Bethy?"

"Sheet music," Beth replied. "You know that, Marmee."

"Exactly," Marmee said. "And it's music you should give back to them."

"But how?" Beth asked.

"Beth can't go over to Aunt March's and play the sheet music for the O'Neills," Jo said. "Aunt March doesn't have a piano."

"And even if she did, I can't really see Aunt March inviting the O'Neills into her parlor for a recital," Meg said. "She may believe in democracy, but that doesn't include socializing with her servants."

"That doesn't mean *we* can't socialize with her servants," Marmee said. "And we have a piano. Beth will invite the O'Neill family — Mrs. O'Neill, Sean, Kathleen, and Maggie — for supper. And after we eat, Beth can play the music for them. For all of us."

"Could I, Marmee?" Beth asked. "Do we have food enough for all the O'Neills?"

"Do we have room enough?" Amy asked.

Marmee laughed. "We've had more people than that over at one time," she said. "And we can certainly feed them. Perhaps not as magnificently as Aunt March could, but Hannah and I know how to cook simple, hearty fare. You invite them, Bethy, and Hannah and I will see to it there's plenty to eat."

"Should I invite them for tomorrow?" Beth asked.

Marmee pursed her lips in thought. "Invite them for Thursday," she said. "Your father will be home by then, and I'm sure he'd like to be here. And you need time to practice the music so you can play it well."

"Thursday, then," Beth said. "Jo, I don't need you to come with me to talk to the O'Neills. But thank you for calling on Mr. Laurence with me."

Jo laughed. "You're welcome, I suppose," she said. "But I don't know that I did you much good."

"You always do me good," Beth said. She gave Marmee a quick kiss. "I'll be back before supper, I promise."

"We'll wait for you," Marmee assured her.

Beth ran all the way to Aunt March's. She'd never been so happy to go there before.

She didn't even bother going to the front door, but went to the servants' entrance by the kitchen. Mrs. O'Neill let her in.

"Thank you, thank you!" Beth cried as soon as she saw Mrs. O'Neill. "I love the music so much. It was very kind of you to give it to me. Thank you!"

Mrs. O'Neill smiled broadly. "It was my

Sean who thought of it," she said. "So it should be him you thank."

"I will," Beth promised. "But I needed to see you first to thank you and to invite you and Sean and Maggie and Kathleen for supper Thursday evening."

Mrs. O'Neill looked shocked. "Your house for supper?" she asked. "Does your mother know of this?"

"It was her idea," Beth said. "Do say you'll come, Mrs. O'Neill. I want you to hear the music you gave me."

"We'd love to, I'm sure," Mrs. O'Neill said. "If Mrs. March will allow us."

"I'll get her permission right now," Beth said. "And then I'll thank Sean, and then I'll go home and have supper with my family, and then I'll start practicing the music you gave me. I want to play it perfectly for you on Thursday."

"We'll hear it as perfect no matter how many mistakes you make," Mrs. O'Neill declared. "You play like an angel, because that's what you are."

"I don't think so," Beth said with a smile. "But I do try to be good. Now I'll talk to Aunt March, and then to Sean, and then I'll see you on Thursday."

"Thursday it is," Mrs. O'Neill said. "And a pleasure it will be."

"For all of us," Beth said. Impulsively she gave Mrs. O'Neill a hug, and then she scurried out of the kitchen to search for Aunt March.

C H A P T E R   8

"There's a package for you, Beth," Hannah said when Beth returned home from school on Tuesday.

"There is?" Beth asked. "I hope it's not from the O'Neills. They can't afford to give me anything more than they already have."

"Open it and see," said Jo.

"It's just an envelope again," Amy said. "I wish one of those presents were something really splendid."

"They've been splendid enough for me," said Beth. She eagerly took the envelope from Hannah and opened it.

"It's two pieces of sheet music," Beth said, pulling them out of the envelope.

"And this time there are two notes," Jo said. "Who are they from, Bethy?"

Beth read the first note.

Dear Beth,

After your visit yesterday, it occurred to me you could only benefit from some new sheet music.

A young lady must have as many advantages as possible if she is to make a good match. Practice your piano daily.

Your loving

Aunt March

"It's always about marrying well with her," Jo said. "Still, it was nice of her to send you some new music."

"Who is the second sheet from?" Meg asked.

"Maybe it's from Beth's future husband," said Amy. "Whoever he might be."

"I don't think so," Beth said, pulling out the

second note. "Not unless you think I'll be marrying Mr. Laurence!"

The girls and Hannah all laughed. "What
does the note say?" Jo asked. "I don't suppose it's an invitation for me to use his
library?"

"I'm afraid not," Beth said, then read the
note aloud.

Dear Beth,

*I fear I was short-tempered with you and
your sister yesterday. You caught me at a very
bad time, and I have never been known for my
patience.*

*Please forgive my rudeness. It was a pleasure
to meet you at Mrs. March's the day before.
Music has brought me much joy over the years,
and I hope this small gift will bring you happi-
ness as well.*

Sincerely,

John Laurence

"How nice of him!" Jo exclaimed. "He isn't
an old bear after all."

"Now I have to thank both of them again," Beth said. "Everybody's being so nice to me, but I feel as though I've spent half my life thanking people!"

"Thanking them for what?" Marmee asked as she came through the front door.

"Aunt March and Mr. Laurence both sent Beth sheet music," Meg said.

"Oh, no," Marmee said. "They didn't!"

"They certainly did," Jo said.

Marmee laughed. "Beth, you are going to have to give a concert recital," she said. "I stopped at Mr. Marshall's this afternoon while I was running my errands and selected a piece of sheet music for you as well."

"Oh, Marmee!" Beth said, running to her mother and embracing her. "You didn't have to do that."

"Apparently not," Marmee said with a laugh. "But it did seem like a good idea at the time."

"Now I have four new pieces of music," Beth said, looking at each sheet happily. "I must make sure I know which one the

O'Neills gave me, so I don't play someone else's piece by mistake Thursday night."

"Why don't we guarantee there'll be no mistakes?" Marmee said. "We could invite Aunt March and Mr. Laurence over for supper as well."

"Would they accept our invitation?" Meg asked. "I've never met Mr. Laurence, but it's hard for me to imagine Aunt March eating with her servants."

"At worst, they'll say no," Marmee said. "And it will be their loss if they do."

Beth stood there thinking. "Marmee, I think it would be very nice to invite Aunt March and Mr. Laurence," she said. "But twenty-five cents couldn't possibly mean as much to them as it does to the O'Neills."

"Do you think we shouldn't invite them, then?" Marmee asked. "The gifts were for you, Beth, so it's your decision."

Beth pictured herself playing for Aunt March and Mr. Laurence. The thought frightened her, but it seemed easier to play the piano for them than to actually talk to them.

"Let's invite them," she said. "But I'd still like to do something special for Sean and his family."

"I have a thought," Jo said. "Sean is always whistling, isn't he?"

"Always," Beth said. "Except at school, of course."

"Do you think you could figure out the tune he whistles on the piano?" Jo asked. "Then after you play all the different pieces, you could play Sean's tune as a special treat for the O'Neills."

"I think I could," Beth said. She walked over to the piano and began to work out the tune.

"That's it," Jo said. "I wonder what the words are."

"Maybe Sean will teach them to us Thursday evening," Marmee said. "I'm sure he and his family will be very pleased that Beth has gone to the effort to learn the song just for them."

"There's so much to do," Beth said, staring at the music. "First I should invite Mr. Laurence and Aunt March."

But before she had the chance to get up from the piano stool, there was a knock on the front door. Hannah opened it, and Mr. Marshall walked in.

"Mr. Marshall," Marmee said. "Did I leave something at your shop?"

"It was I who left something," he said. "Beth, after your call yesterday, I thought about what Jo said."

Amy nudged Jo. "What did you say this time?"

"Nothing bad," Jo said. "Did I, Mr. Marshall?"

"Absolutely not," Mr. Marshall declared. "All Jo did was point out that I owe Beth a debt of gratitude for speaking to her aunt for me. I meant to give you a piece of sheet music to bring to Beth, Mrs. March, but I forgot. Nowadays I'm forgetting everything, including my manners. And then, after you left, I thought about how the O'Neills had bought Beth a piece of sheet music, and Mr. Laurence, and your aunt, and you, Mrs. March. That's the same as Beth buying four pieces herself. And my offer is, buy four pieces and get one free. So here are two new pieces of sheet music for you, Beth. One from me as a thank-you and one as part of my sale price." He handed the two pieces to Beth with a flourish.

"Now you'll have to give two concert recitals," Jo said. "How wonderful, Beth."

"Thank you, Mr. Marshall," Beth said. "Marmee, may I?"

"There's always room for one more," Marmee said with a smile.

"Mr. Marshall, we're having a supper party on Thursday," Beth said. "The O'Neills have already accepted, and we're going to invite Mr. Laurence and Aunt March. After supper, I'm going to play the music everybody gave me. Would you care to join us?"

"I'd like that a great deal," Mr. Marshall replied. "Thank you, Beth, for the invitation."

Beth smiled. "I'd better go over to Mr. Laurence's and Aunt March's right away," she said. "And tell them about the social event of the season!"

CHAPTER 9

"What an excellent meal," Mr. Laurence declared Thursday evening. "Mrs. March, you and Hannah are fine cooks."

"Hannah is, I know," Marmee replied.

Hannah had joined the family, the O'Neills, Aunt March, Mr. Laurence, and Mr. Marshall for supper. Beth and Jo had set the table and served the food, with Meg and Amy helping.

Beth couldn't remember ever seeing so many people seated around the table. Even though she knew almost everyone, and even though Mr. Laurence wasn't too frightening when surrounded by others, she hadn't said very much. But it hadn't mattered. The supper had been accompanied by lively conversation and some friendly political debate.

"This has been a truly excellent evening," Father said. "Good food, good company, good conversation. What more could a person ask for?"

"Good weather," piped up Amy, and everyone laughed. It had rained all day.

"How is your rheumatism, Aunt March?" Father asked. "I know it's always bad in this sort of weather."

Aunt March harrumphed. "I've been better," she said. "But there's been so much chattering, I've hardly had a chance to feel it."

"Perhaps we've found a treatment for pain," said Mr. Marshall. "Supper with six adults and seven children."

"Pain might be preferable," grumbled Aunt March, but even Beth could tell she was joking.

"I'm looking forward to Beth's performance," said Mr. Laurence. "It's been quite a while since I've heard any new songs."

"Beth's been practicing and practicing," said Jo. "You're in for quite a treat."

"Perhaps we should begin," suggested Father. "Beth, are you ready for your performance?"

For a moment Beth wished she were anywhere else than her own parlor. She had rehearsed as much as she could, but school took up most of her time, and six new pieces of music and one song from memory were a lot to learn.

"I don't know how well I'll do," she said softly.

"We won't hear the mistakes," Jo said. "Just the songs."

Beth smiled. Sometimes Jo knew just what to say to her. She walked over to the piano and arranged the music sheets.

"This song is called 'Listen to the Mockingbird,' " she said. "I think it's very pretty. You can almost hear the mockingbird in the music."

She played the song all the way through, stumbling only once. Everyone applauded when she finished.

"The words are really pretty, too," Meg said. Beth played the song again, and this time Meg sang along.

"Two such talented lasses," said Mrs. O'Neill. "Truly this is a blessed family."

"That it is, Mrs. O'Neill," Father said. "Beth, I can't remember when I've heard a song I liked so much. You must play it for us tomorrow night, and Meg will have to teach us all the words. Not that anyone is likely to mistake me for a mockingbird."

"You're more a proud eagle," said Marmee. "I've never heard you mock."

"My wife thinks I'm a paragon," Father said.

"Your wife is a paragon," said Mr. Marshall.

"And what might a paragon be?" Sean asked.

"Sean, hush," said his mother.

"That's how a man learns, Mam," Sean said. "By questioning what he doesn't know."

Mr. Marshall nodded. "Mrs. O'Neill, my own family had very little money," he said. "My father died when I was quite young, and my mother had to work to support my brothers and me. But she was determined that her children would be educated. Now one of my brothers is a lawyer and the other a teacher."

"And you are a man of great learning yourself," Father said. "I'm always impressed by the breadth of your knowledge."

"That means a great deal coming from you," Mr. Marshall said. "And Mrs. O'Neill, most of what I know I learned by asking."

"See, Mam?" Sean said. He turned to Mr. Marshall. "What is a paragon?"

"A paragon is a truly excellent person," Mr. Marshall said.

"Then it's Miss Bethy who's the paragon," said Sean.

"Hear, hear!" said Jo.

Beth blushed. It was almost harder to be praised than to play for so many people.

"Beth, what song will you play next?" Marmee asked.

Beth smiled gratefully at her mother. "This song isn't really meant for springtime," she said. "But it's very jolly. It's called 'Jingle Bells.'"

"I know that one!" Meg exclaimed. "Mary Howe taught it to us at a Christmas party this year. Play it, Beth, and I'll sing along."

Beth began to play, and Meg's sweet soprano made the song even prettier.

> *Jingle bells, jingle bells*
> *Jingle all the way*
> *Oh, what fun it is to ride*
> *In a one-horse open sleigh!*

"That is a jolly song!" Jo said. "Play it again, Beth, and we can all sing along."

And indeed they all did. Even Aunt March joined in, although when they finished, she grumbled something about how uncomfortable open sleighs could be on a cold winter's day.

"But romantic as well," Mr. Laurence said. "Huddling together under a fur wrap."

"Mr. Laurence!" Aunt March said, but then she smiled.

Beth couldn't believe it. Was it possible Aunt March had known romance? She tried to remember Uncle March, but it was hard to picture him as a young man, and the very idea of Aunt March's ever having been young made Beth dizzy.

"Play the other songs, Beth," said Amy, and Beth did. Some of the songs had been easier to learn than the others, and at least one of them gave even Meg some trouble to sing. But Beth played them all, and each time, everyone applauded.

"I have another song I've learned," she said, once she'd played the six new pieces that had been given to her. "I'm playing this one by ear, so if I don't get all the notes right, you'll have to forgive me."

"As though you could do anything that needs forgiveness," said Mrs. O'Neill.

Beth began playing the song Sean always whistled.

"Do you hear that, Mam?" Sean asked.

"Remember how we'd sing that in the old country?"

Mrs. O'Neill began to cry. "It brings back many memories," she said. "But all the times I've heard it, never once have I heard it played on a piano."

"Only on the fiddle," Sean said. "Remember the fiddler, Maggie?"

Maggie nodded. "He was a handsome lad."

"Maggie was sweet on him," Kathleen said. "Were you not, Maggie?"

"All the lasses were," Maggie said.

"The lasses and the ladies," Mrs. O'Neill added, and then she laughed. Beth realized she'd never heard Mrs. O'Neill laugh.

Sean looked at Beth. "Thank you," he whispered. " 'Tis quite a gift you've blessed us with."

Beth played the song again, her heart full of joy. She knew then with absolute certainty that the very best gifts were the ones that could be shared.

PORTRAITS OF
LITTLE WOMEN
ACTIVITIES

DILL POPOVERS

Dill is an herb that adds a delicious fragrance and tasty seasoning to popovers.

INGREDIENTS
1 cup white flour
$1/4$ teaspoon salt
2 large eggs
1 cup milk
$1/2$ teaspoon dill weed (if using fresh dill, use 1 tablespoon)
2 tablespoons melted butter, divided

Preheat oven to 400 degrees.
1. In a medium bowl mix the flour and salt. Set aside.
2. In a small bowl beat the eggs thoroughly with the milk and dill weed.
3. Stir in 1 tablespoon of the melted butter.
4. Gradually stir the egg mixture into the flour mixture until smooth (see note).
5. Use the remaining 1 tablespoon melted butter to grease 10 large muffin cups.
6. Fill each muffin cup halfway with the batter.
7. Bake 30 to 40 minutes, or until puffed and golden.

Serve the popovers warm with a hearty soup or a luncheon salad, or with tea in the afternoon.

NOTE: This batter may be made in a blender by whirling all ingredients at high speed for 20 seconds.

SHEET MUSIC DÉCOUPAGE

Display this découpage as a wall hanging or on a small picture easel as a table decoration.

MATERIALS

1 piece of sheet music (the older the paper the better)

1 piece of découpage wood at least 6 by 9 inches but not larger than 8 by 10 inches. This may be purchased at any craft store. Buy one already stained the color of your choice.

2 cups cold strong coffee (or strong tea)

1 piece of aluminum foil twice the size of the
  wood piece being used
1 bottle white craft glue
1-inch paintbrush
1 miniature musical instrument, preferably a
  violin (bought at a craft store)
3 sprigs dried statice
6 small silk flowers with leaves, such as roses,
  pansies, or mums, not more than 1 inch wide

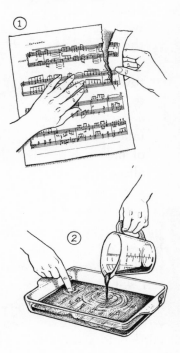

1. Tear ragged edges
   around the sheet
   of music so that it
   measures about 1
   inch smaller, on all
   sides, than the
   piece of wood you
   have selected. This
   measurement
   shouldn't be exact,
   but should have a
   frayed and jagged
   look.
2. Put the two cups
   of cold coffee or
   tea into a shallow
   container that will
   allow you to soak

the sheet of music flat. This process will color the paper and make it look old and will give the frayed edges a worn look. Soak for about 10 minutes. When you're satisfied with the color, roll the sheet of music in a piece of paper towel and allow it to dry for 15 minutes. Unroll, take out the sheet of music, and allow it to air dry. Don't be concerned if it curls.

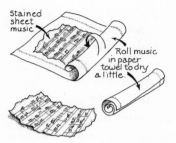

Stained sheet music

Roll music in paper towel to dry a little.

3. Lay down the sheet of aluminum foil, place the wood piece on it, and apply several coats of craft glue by

③

GLUE

following the label
directions. Allow to
dry. (NOTE: Keep
a glass with warm
soapy water next to
your project, along
with a piece of
paper towel. Each
time you finish a
step with the glue
brush, put it into
the water; towel-
dry it before using
again.)

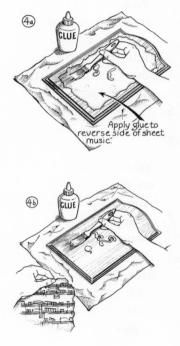

4a. Place the sheet of
music bottom side
up on top of the
wood piece and
coat thoroughly
with craft glue.

4b. Lift the music
and apply another
layer of craft glue
to the wood
surface. Place the
wet side of the

music on the wet wood. Allow to dry thoroughly.

5. Apply one or two coats of craft glue to the top of the sheet music and wood. Allow to dry. Make sure you apply it so that all edges are fixed to the wood's surface.

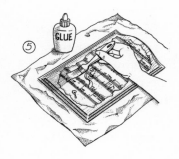

6. Take the miniature violin, apply some craft glue to the back, and place it on the découpage. Allow to dry.

7. Arrange the statice, silk flowers, and leaves around the violin. Use small dabs of glue to keep all items fluffed up

Glue violin onto sheet music.

and as natural as possible.

The découpage looks equally pretty when you use any kind of printed paper.

ABOUT THE AUTHOR OF
PORTRAITS OF LITTLE WOMEN

SUSAN BETH PFEFFER is the author of both middle-grade and young adult fiction. Her middle-grade novels include *Nobody's Daughter* and its companion, *Justice for Emily*. Her highly praised *The Year Without Michael* is an ALA Best Book for Young Adults, an ALA YALSA Best of the Best, and a *Publishers Weekly* Best Book of the Year. Her novels for young adults include *Twice Taken*, *Most Precious Blood*, *About David*, and *Family of Strangers*. Susan Beth Pfeffer lives in Middletown, New York.

A WORD ABOUT
LOUISA MAY ALCOTT

LOUISA MAY ALCOTT was born in 1832 in Germantown, Pennsylvania, and grew up in the Boston-Concord area of Massachusetts. She received her early education from her father, Bronson Alcott, a renowned educator and writer, who eventually left teaching to study philosophy. To supplement the family income, Louisa worked as a teacher, a household servant, and a seamstress, and she wrote stories as well as poems for newspapers and magazines. In 1868 she published the first volume of *Little Women,* a novel about four sisters growing up in a small New England town during the Civil War. The immediate success of *Little Women* made Louisa May Alcott a celebrated writer, and the novel remains one of today's best-loved books. Alcott wrote until her death in 1888.